HEROES IN TRAINING

Hercules and the Nine-Headed Hydra

By Tracey West

Created by
Joan Holub and Suzanne Williams

Aladdin

NEW YORK   LONDON   TORONTO   SYDNEY   NEW DELHI

This book is a work of fiction. Any references to historical events, real people, or real places are used fictitiously. Other names, characters, places, and events are products of the author's imagination, and any resemblance to actual events or places or persons, living or dead, is entirely coincidental.

ALADDIN

An imprint of Simon & Schuster Children's Publishing Division
1230 Avenue of the Americas, New York, NY 10020
First Aladdin paperback edition December 2019
Text copyright © 2019 by Joan Holub and Suzanne Williams
Illustrations copyright © 2019 by Craig Phillips
Also available in an Aladdin hardcover edition.

ALADDIN and related logo are registered trademarks of Simon & Schuster, Inc.
For information about special discounts for bulk purchases, please contact Simon & Schuster Special Sales at 1-866-506-1949 or business@simonandschuster.com.
The Simon & Schuster Speakers Bureau can bring authors to your live event. For more information or to book an event contact the Simon & Schuster Speakers Bureau at 1-866-248-3049 or visit our website at www.simonspeakers.com.
Series designed by Karin Paprocki
Interior designed by Mike Rosamilia
The text of this book was set in Adobe Garamond Pro.
Manufactured in the United States of America 1019 OFF
2 4 6 8 10 9 7 5 3 1
Library of Congress Control Number 2019937840
ISBN 978-1-5344-3292-5 (hc)
ISBN 978-1-5344-3291-8 (pbk)
ISBN 978-1-5344-3293-2 (eBook)

⚡ Contents ⚡

Hercules and the Nine-Headed Hydra

Greetings,
Mortal Readers,

Wow, that sounds serious, doesn't it? But that's how Pythia, the Oracle of Delphi, told me I have to begin these messages. And since I am learning how to be an oracle too, I've got to do it.

This story's intense, so let us commence! Things have really changed in Greece. The young Olympians (including me, Apollo) battled King Cronus and the Titans. It was an epic battle with monsters and giant immortals and an enormous dragon. Winning seemed impossible, but we did it!

Then Zeus, our leader, took over the throne on Mount Olympus, and the rest of us Olympians had to find something else to do besides battle Titans. We are scattered around Greece, and everything is strangely calm now that King Cronus is defeated.

But Pythia told me that something is coming to change things. She told me to look into the future. When I try to see the future, I hear rhymes in my head. And this is what I heard: *Beware the boy who challenges thunder. He'll tear the Olympians asunder!*

In case you don't know, "asunder" means "apart." That sounds pretty scary, but I know that we Olympians are strong. *Nothing* can stop us when we stick together.

In the meantime, I'll have to keep an eye out for this boy. . . .

Catch you later, gladiator! (Hmm. That's not a perfect sign-off, but I'll work on it!)

CHAPTER ONE

The Chicken Dilemma

A single peacock feather floated up from the Greek village. It flew up into the sky, all the way to the top of Mount Olympus. When the feather reached the snow-covered peak, it flew through the entrance of the shiny marble temple.

The feather soared into the royal throne room and settled in the hand of a girl with long blond hair. She stared into the shimmering blue, green, and gold eye design on the feather. Then she turned to the boy on the throne.

"Hermes is bringing two more villagers to see you, Zeus," she informed him.

The boy sighed. "Another problem, Hera? What is it this time? I'm getting kind of tired of listening to all these boring problems."

Hera smirked. "Well, you wanted to be charge," she said.

"Hey, that's not fair!" Zeus replied. "It's not my fault that I was chosen by fate to lead the Olympians. I mean, I do *want* to be in charge, but it's not like I asked for it."

"Mm-hm," Hera said with a frown.

"What does that mean?" Zeus asked.

Hera shrugged. "I get it about the destiny and everything, but you can step down at any time. I'm sure there are others who wouldn't mind being in charge."

Others like you, you mean, Zeus thought. He and his sister were a lot alike. They were both ten years old. They both had blue eyes. And they were both natural leaders. Hera had always thought *she* should have been chosen to sit on the throne, not Zeus.

Zeus sighed and felt for Bolt, the lightning bolt–shaped dagger tucked into his belt. Pythia, the Oracle of Delphi, had given him the magical tool at the start of his journey as a hero in training. He hadn't used Bolt in a long time—not since the Olympians won the battle against the Titans.

"Incoming!" Hera cried.

A boy with dark hair flew into the throne room, powered by magical winged sandals. Under each arm he held a man from the village—a tall one and a short one. He landed and released the men.

"Whew!" Hermes exclaimed. "Two at a time is tough!"

Both men bowed to Zeus. The shorter man, Zeus noticed, had a white chicken tucked into his jacket.

"What kind of problem do you guys have that is so important you need to ask me?" Zeus asked them.

The man with the chicken spoke. "Idas is trying to steal my chicken!"

"That's a lie!" cried the other man. "Enops stole *my* chicken and won't give it back!"

"A chicken?" Zeus asked. "You want me to solve a problem about a chicken?"

Enops bowed again. "Yes, mighty Zeus!"

Zeus hated these problems. When he'd been fighting the Titans, he'd had real problems—like how to defeat birds with poisonous poop or hungry half-giants. In those cases, Zeus had had two main solutions: fight, or run away.

"Um, maybe you two guys should fight," Zeus said, unsure. "Whoever wins gets to keep the chicken."

"Yes!" Idas cheered, but Enops looked afraid.

Hera rolled her eyes at Zeus. "Are you serious, Boltbrain?" she hissed in his ear. "Nobody needs to get hurt over a chicken."

She stepped in front of the throne. "I have a better idea," she said. "Enops, put the chicken on the floor between you. Whoever the chicken goes to is the rightful owner."

Enops frowned, but he liked that plan better than fighting Idas. He placed the chicken on the floor of the throne room.

"Cluck!" The chicken flapped her stubby wings and threw herself out the window.

"Can chickens fly?" Zeus wondered.

"On it!" Hermes cried, and he flew out the window after the chicken.

"Well, I guess that settles it," Hera said. "The chicken doesn't want to be with either of you. The mighty Zeus has spoken."

She nudged Zeus. He nodded. "Oh, right! I have spoken," he said.

"You're welcome," Hera muttered.

"Hey, I didn't ask you to help," Zeus said. "I thought my idea was pretty good. More exciting, anyway."

Enops and Idas looked at each other and shrugged.

"Oh well," Idas said. "At least we got to see the palace. It's pretty cool up here."

"Yeah," Enops agreed. "Hey, where's Hercules?"

"Who?" Zeus asked.

"Hercules," Enops repeated, pronouncing it

"her-cue-leeze." "That kid who single-handedly took down the Titans."

"Are you kidding me?" Zeus asked. "Who does this Hercules guy think he is?"

"Where did you hear that?" Hera asked.

"Everyone in Greece is talking about it," Idas chimed in. "The Olympians couldn't defeat the Titans, so Hercules showed up and saved the day!"

Zeus's eyes flashed. "That's a lie!" he said. A low rumble of thunder rolled through the palace. "The Olympians fought a long, hard battle against the Titans. We worked together, and we sent King Cronus and everyone who stood with him to a prison in the Underworld!"

Hermes flew back through the window, holding the chicken.

"Take these men back to the village!" Zeus boomed. "And leave the chicken!"

Hermes dropped the chicken, which flew onto Zeus's lap. Then he picked up Enops and Idas and flew out of the palace.

"That was strange," Hera said. "Have you ever heard of this Hercules guy?"

Zeus shook his head. "No. But whoever he is, he's a liar."

Hera nodded. "Sounds like it."

Zeus slumped in his throne, cradling his new chicken. "It's not fair," he said. "We spent months traveling, hungry, cold, and scared. We risked our lives fighting monsters. And it's like nobody remembers that! And on top of it all, I'm stuck on this dumb throne solving dumb problems. And it's not even comfy!"

"Well, like I said . . . ," Hera began.

"Yeah, I know. I was chosen," Zeus said. "But I have the most boring job! Poseidon is ruling the seas, and Hades is ruling the Underworld. Apollo and Dionysus are hanging out in the temple at Delphi, jamming together and holding contests. Demeter and Hestia are traveling all around Greece, helping people. Artemis gets to live in the forest, and Aphrodite gets to live at the beach. Even Hephaestus and Ares are having fun building machines in a cool new volcano."

"Well, Hermes, Athena, and I stayed here to help you," Hera said. Then she lowered her voice. "Although I'm wondering if we should have."

Zeus heard her and sighed again. "I'm glad that you guys are helping me," he said. "It's just . . . I miss the adventures, you know? Even though they were dangerous."

Hera nodded. "I understand."

His eyes flashed again. "And now this

Hercules guy! Taking credit for what *we* did! If I ever meet this kid in person, I'll—"

Hermes flew into the throne room, carrying a boy under one arm.

"Presenting Hercules!"

CHAPTER TWO

Hercules the Mighty . . . Liar

Zeus stood up in his chair.

Squawk! The chicken tumbled off his lap.

Zeus glared at the blond-haired boy, who wore a fancy tunic trimmed in gold. "Are you the same Hercules who's telling everybody that you defeated the Titans all by yourself?" Zeus asked.

The boy held up his hands. "Whoa, simmer

down, dude," Hercules said. "I would never say anything like that!"

Hera stared at him with narrowed eyes and folded her arms across her chest. "So why did those men from the village tell us that everyone is saying that you took down King Cronus and the Titans?"

Hercules grinned and ran a hand through his thick, wavy blond hair. "I think it has something to do with my naturally heroic appearance," he boasted. "People look at me and assume I'm a god. But they're only half-right."

"What do you mean?" Zeus asked.

"Well, I'm half-immortal, on my dad's side," Hercules replied. "So, you know, when word of that gets around, people talk. They even gave me a nickname: Hercules the Mighty."

"Mighty liar, you mean," Hera muttered.

Zeus studied the boy. He didn't necessarily

look like a god, but neither did he or any of the other Olympians. To be honest, Zeus thought, Hercules might even look more like a god than any of them, with his perfect hair and muscles.

"If you're half-immortal, you must have powers," Zeus said.

Hercules flexed his arm. "I sure do. Super-strength!"

"Really?" Hera asked. "Prove it, then!"

"Sure!" Hercules said, and he strolled over to Zeus's throne. He placed a hand underneath it. "I can lift this throne with one . . ."

He placed his other hand under the throne. "I can lift this throne!" he said, and he tried to lift it, grunting. "What is this made of, solid marble or something?"

"Yes," Zeus replied.

"Well, I mean, that's a pretty tall order,"

Hercules said. "I'm only *half*-immortal, after all. What else can I pick up?"

He turned to Hera and moved toward her. She held up both hands.

"Do not even think about it," she warned.

Zeus frowned. This Hercules guy was obviously a big liar. But he seemed pretty harmless. *I can probably threaten him with a thunderbolt and he'll stop lying,* Zeus reasoned. *Then I'll never have to see him again.*

"Anyway, I can't help it if people think I'm awesome," Hercules went on. "They used to think you were awesome too, but now that you're spending all your time up here on Mount Olympus, they sometimes forget about you."

"But they remember me when they need help with their silly problems," Zeus pointed out. Then he realized something. "Is that why you're here? Do you need me to solve a problem for you?"

15

"Well, I'm not the one with the problem," Hercules said. "It's the king of Argos."

"Argos? That's in the north of Greece, right?" Hera asked.

"That's right," Hercules replied. "Anyway, Eurystheus is kind of an old dude, but he's like my third cousin or something. And my mom sent me to visit him and he's, like, just no fun, you know? Like, he always makes me eat my vegetables and wants me to do dumb chores like clean his chicken coop. A really bossy guy!"

"So what exactly do you want me to do about it?" Zeus asked. "Why don't you just leave? I mean, it looks like you've left him already."

"Well, that wasn't the problem, exactly," Hercules went on. His eyes darted around the throne room, avoiding Zeus's gaze. "I was cleaning his chicken coop the other day, and it's possible that some of the eggs might have accidentally slipped out of my hands, and because of my superstrength they went flying toward the palace, and they broke on the palace walls, and egg got all over the place."

"Accidentally? You egged the guy's palace by mistake?" Hera asked.

Hercules held up his palms. "I swear, I just can't control my strength sometimes. My massive muscles sent those eggs flying! And boy, was Eurystheus mad! He started yelling and screaming at me and threatening all kinds of stuff."

"Like what?" Zeus asked.

"Oh, like waging war, total destruction, massive army of soldiers, something like that," Hercules replied. "I'm not sure exactly, because that's about when I started running away as fast as I could."

"That sounds like a problem, all right," Zeus said. "Good luck solving it."

Hercules frowned. "You mean you won't help me?"

"No!" Zeus exclaimed. "Why should I? It's about time people started learning how to solve their own problems."

Suddenly a sound rumbled through the throne room.

"Calm down with the thunder, Bolt Boy," Hera said.

"That wasn't me," Zeus said.

Hera went to the window and looked out. "Well, that's interesting," she said. "There's, like, an army down there."

Zeus frowned. "You mean, like soldiers?"

Hera nodded. "Yeah, a whole bunch of them. That's the sound of them marching toward Olympus."

Hermes flew into the throne room. "Zeus, there's an army marching toward us! Their leader is climbing up the mountain, and he's really angry. I tried to stop him, but he said if I put one hand on him, he would order his army to attack."

Zeus looked at Hercules. "Is there any chance this is that king you were telling me about? The angry one with the soldiers?"

As he spoke, a man wearing a red tunic, with a bushy beard and a crown on his head, stomped into the throne room.

"Surrender, gods of Olympus!" he bellowed.

CHAPTER THREE

The Angry King

Zeus's hand flew to Bolt.

"Surrender? Who are you, and why are you waging war against us?" Zeus demanded to know.

"You are giving safe harbor to your brother Hercules!" the man bellowed. "Hercules, the egger of palaces!"

"He is not my brother," Zeus protested. He

looked at Hercules. "Did you tell him I was your brother?"

Hercules shrugged. "Well, it's possible. I mean, I *am* half god on my father's side, and I don't know who he was, so we could be related."

Zeus shook his head. "You never tell the truth, do you?"

Hercules didn't answer. Zeus turned to the angry king. "You're Eurystheus, right? Of Argos?"

"That is *King* Eurystheus, young man!" the king boomed.

"Right," Zeus said. "Listen, I know you have a problem with Hercules, but that is between the two of you. He is not my brother, and I never even met him until a few minutes ago."

"But he egged my palace!" the king protested.

"Maybe he did, and maybe he didn't," Zeus said. "That's your problem, not mine."

The king's face was turning purple with anger. He pointed at Hercules. "Look! He's holding an egg right now!"

Hercules was, somehow, holding a white egg in his hand.

"That chicken just laid it," he said, pointing to the hen, who was exploring the throne room. "I wasn't going to let a good egg go to waste."

"See? He was going to egg me!" the king shouted.

"Maybe I was going to eat it," Hercules argued. "You can't prove anything."

"He probably stole that chicken from me too," King Eurystheus complained.

Zeus groaned. "Not the chicken again. Hermes, get her out of here!"

"Sure thing, boss!" Hermes said. He scooped up the chicken and plucked the egg out of Hercules's hand before he flew out of the throne room.

"King Eurystheus, there is no reason for you to attack Olympus," Zeus said sternly. "So if you don't mind, why don't you and Hercules leave and figure this out yourselves."

The king scowled. "You haven't proven to me that he is *not* your brother," he said. "Besides, I brought my army all the way here from Argos. They'll be upset if I don't let them attack something."

"Seriously? Just tell them to retreat. You're a king, aren't you?" Zeus challenged him.

"Yes I am," the king shot back. "Which is why you have no right to tell me what to do."

Zeus motioned to the throne behind him. "I'm the ruler of the Olympians!"

"Well, you're not the boss of me," the king replied. "King Cronus, well, he was an impressive giant. I listened to him. But you're just a little boy in a chair that's too big for you."

Zeus's eyes flashed. "Bolt, large!" he commanded, and Bolt grew until it was three times taller than Zeus. The lightning bolt sparked with electricity.

Hera touched his arm. "Settle down, Thunderpants!"

"I do *not* want a war!" Zeus thundered at King Eurystheus and Hercules. Then he took a deep breath. "I mean, sure, fighting is exciting and gets your heart pounding and everything. But people get hurt when there's a war. And there's no reason for people to get hurt because of some broken eggs. That doesn't make any sense."

Suddenly a golden-haired boy appeared out

of nowhere, playing a lyre. He strummed on its strings and sang.

"Pythia sensed that you were in trouble, so she sent me here on the double!"

CHAPTER FOUR

The Oracle Speaks

I can handle this, Apollo," Zeus told the golden-haired boy.

"Yeah, he's doing a great job," Hera said. "We're about to go to war with this guy." She pointed to King Eurystheus.

The king pumped his fist in the air. "One word from me, and my soldiers will attack!"

"See what I mean?" Hera asked.

Apollo began to strum on his instrument.

"Your Highness, please don't scream and shout," he sang. *"Let's talk and work something out."*

The lyre was Apollo's magical object—just like Hera's peacock feather and Zeus's Bolt. When he played, whatever he sang about would come true.

The king's face softened. "I suppose we could talk," he said.

Hera stepped forward. "Good! I think I have a solution," she said. "Maybe Hercules could perform some tasks to make up for the mess he caused. You know, like he could clean up the eggshells."

"The eggs he threw were the eggs of Stymphalian birds," King Eurystheus pointed out. "They destroyed my castle!"

Zeus remembered facing the Stymphalian birds on his quest to find Ares, another Olympian. The birds had metal feathers and deadly, poisonous poop. He wasn't surprised to hear that their eggs could destroy a palace.

Zeus turned to Hercules. "I thought you said the eggs *accidentally* flew out of your hands when you were cleaning the *chicken* coop."

Hercules shrugged. "Hey, I don't know how those Stymphalian eggs got in there. Maybe the birds were hanging out with the chickens."

"Okay, that's different, but maybe he could do some other tasks," Hera suggested. "Something to make things right."

"He could be my servant for the rest of his life!" the king said. "I'd like that."

"No way!" Hercules protested. "That's not fair. I'm a hero. I'll perform some kind of heroic deed and then we'll be even."

"What kind of heroic deed?" Zeus wanted to know.

Hercules shrugged. "I don't know. I'll just wait for something to come up."

"That's too easy," King Eurystheus said. "What if nothing ever comes up? You need to pay for what you did to me."

Apollo interrupted. "What if we let the oracle decide on what the task is?" he suggested. "We can go there now, and whatever the oracle says is final."

"Hmm," said the king. "That does sound fair."

"Final, no matter what the oracle says?" Hercules asked.

Apollo nodded. "Yes. It's the only fair way."

Zeus looked at the king and Hercules. "This is the only fair way," he said. "Apollo, take us to Delphi!"

Apollo's hands flew across the strings of his lyre. *"First we're here; then we're there. Moving*

quickly through the air. In one second we will be,
at the temple of Delphi!"

The magic of the lyre caused them all to disappear from the temple. In the next instant Zeus, Hera, Hercules, King Eurystheus, and Apollo were standing on the marble steps of the temple in Delphi.

Zeus blinked. His head felt a little light from the magical journey. He gazed up at the small, round temple made of gleaming white marble. Memories of his first visit there came rushing back.

Zeus had rushed into the temple, chased by the half-giant warriors known as Cronies. With no weapon to defend himself, he had pulled the jagged-looked dagger from a stone. Pythia, the oracle of the temple, had appeared from the mist and told him that only the trueborn king of the Olympians could have removed the bolt from the stone. That he was a hero in training, destined to sit on the throne someday.

Zeus hadn't been sure if he should believe the woman, who'd thought his name was Goose instead of Zeus, and said her vision of the future was foggy. But she had been right about everything.

Today he heard music coming from inside the temple. They headed inside and saw a kid in a purple tunic and green pants singing and whipping his long, golden-brown hair around his face. Behind him, four men with goat horns and hairy goat legs were banging on drums.

"What in Greece is going on here?" King Eurystheus demanded.

A misty fog rose up inside the temple as they asked the question. A woman with long black hair wearing a hooded robe and spectacles on her eyes appeared from the mist.

"Dionysus, Goat Guys, quiet down," she

told the musicians. "We have visitors."

The drumming stopped. "Sure thing, Pythia!" answered the singing boy.

Pythia turned to Apollo. "You brought everyone here?"

"We had to come here," Apollo said. "Hercules destroyed the king's palace, and we agreed that he has to do a bunch of tasks to make up for it, but we couldn't decide what those tasks should be. We're going to let the oracle tell us."

Pythia looked at the king and Hercules. "He means me. I'm the oracle."

"Can you do it?" Apollo asked.

"I think you should do it, Apollo," Pythia told him. "You have been doing very well in your training. You can see the future clearly because your spectacles don't get fogged up in the mist, like mine do."

Apollo nodded, and Zeus thought he looked

a little nervous. "Okay, I'll give it a shot."

Pythia began to wave her arms around like snakes. More mist shot up from the floor.

"Look into the mist, Apollo," she said. "Tell us what you see."

Zeus watched Apollo as he gazed into the fog. His blue eyes grew wide, and his whole body was very still for a few moments.

Finally Apollo blinked. He played his lyre and sang:

> "*Three tasks must Hercules achieve,*
> *And only then will the king reprieve.*
> *First he must go to the Hydra's cave,*
> *But only if he is strong and brave.*
> *The serpent has nine heads, not one,*
> *And from these heads he must not run.*
> *He must get his hands on the Hydra's tail,*
> *And bring the king one shimmering scale.*"

Everyone was quiet for a moment.

"What does 'reprieve' mean?" Hercules asked.

"It means to stop the punishment," Pythia explained.

The king frowned. "What am I supposed to do with the scale of a sea serpent?"

Zeus shrugged. "Maybe it's made of gold or something."

"Or maybe the idea is just to punish Hercules," Hera guessed. "The Hydra has nine heads, which sounds pretty dangerous. Hercules might not succeed."

A slow smile crept across the king's face. "Punishment. I like that."

"Nine heads?" Hercules asked. "Seriously?"

"What, is that too many heads for Hercules the Mighty?" Zeus asked.

"Then it's settled!" Pythia said. "Hercules shall perform the first task. Then we shall all meet back here in one week to learn the second task."

The mist swirled around her, and she disappeared.

"I am satisfied, for now," King Eurystheus said. "But if Hercules does not bring me that Hydra scale in one week, I am going to attack!"

He stomped out of the temple.

Zeus patted Hercules on the back. "All right, well, good luck with the Hydra thing!"

"Wait, really?" Hercules asked. "I mean, I'm not *afraid* or anything, but doesn't that seem like a pretty big punishment for throwing some eggs?"

"Everyone agreed to abide by the oracle," Apollo reminded him.

Hercules frowned. "How do I even find this Hydra? Can I get more than a week? This is so unfair!"

Zeus led him back outside the temple.

"Good luck, Hercules," Zeus said, and then he stopped.

A crowd of villagers was swarming around the temple.

"It's him! It's Zeus!" someone shouted.

Uh-oh, Zeus thought.

The villagers began to climb up the stairs, all talking at once.

"Zeus, a mouse is eating my grain!"

"Zeus, my neighbor is stealing my milk!"

"Zeus, I have a giant pimple on my back! Can you cure me?"

Zeus quickly pulled Hercules back into the temple. An idea popped into his mind.

"All right, Hercules, I'm going with you," he said. He would rather face a nine-headed serpent than stick around and solve boring problems all day.

Hercules's face lit up. "Excellent! I could use an assistant!"

"Assistant?" Zeus asked. "Now wait one second—"

"Every great adventurer needs a good sidekick," Hercules chatted on. "Hercules and his trusty sidekick, Zeus! I like the sound of that."

Hera grinned at Zeus. "Are you sure you want to go with this guy?" she asked.

Zeus looked at Hercules, who was flexing his arms and admiring his reflection in the marble. Then Zeus looked outside at the crowd of villagers on the stairs. If he stayed here, he'd have to listen to their problems all day long. But if he went with Hercules, there would be fresh air, open spaces, and probably monsters. Even though monsters were frightening, Zeus felt a thrill run through him.

"I'm going to go with Hercules," he said. "Can you handle things here?"

"Do you have to even ask me?" Hera shot back. "Of course I can!"

Zeus nodded and turned to Hercules. "Come on. Let's go get that Hydra scale!"

CHAPTER FIVE

The Angry Bird

T his is the most boring adventure ever," Hercules moaned. "We've been walking for two days, and nothing exciting has happened!"

"You can't have an adventure without walking," Zeus told him. "And it's better than *running* from monsters and Cronies, trust me!"

Zeus was actually enjoying being back out in nature instead of cooped up in the temple on Mount Olympus. Walking at a normal pace allowed him to take in the scenery—green hills dotted with white goats, and meadows of colorful flowers—they had traveled through on their way to the coastline.

Hercules, on the other hand, had done nothing but complain.

"Why couldn't we have had Apollo just sing a song and get us to the Hydra in an instant?" Hercules wanted to know.

"Because, like Apollo said, and like I've explained a *million* times, that wouldn't be fair," Zeus replied. "The whole idea of a task is that it has to be challenging. If it's easy, what's the point?"

"Easy would have been just fine with me," Hercules muttered, kicking a rock on the path in front of him.

"Anyway, we don't have too much farther to

walk," Zeus said. "Another day, maybe."

"A whole day?" Hercules groaned.

"I'll check with Chip," Zeus offered.

Chip was Zeus's second magical object—a stone disc that hung around his neck from a cord. Chip could communicate with Zeus through glowing symbols or letters that appeared on its surface. Chip could also speak, in a unique language called Chip Latin. It was kind of like Pig Latin, only you moved the first letter of each word to the end of the word and added "ip."

"Chip, when will we reach the swamps of Lerna?" Zeus asked, for Apollo had told them that was where they would find the Hydra.

"Orning-mip," Chip replied.

"Morning," Zeus translated. "See? I told you it was about a day."

Hercules reached out to touch Chip, and

Zeus moved his hand away. "I told you, Chip is *my* magical object. So is Bolt. They have to stay with me."

"But can't I at least ask Chip a question?" Hercules asked. "It'll answer me, right?"

Zeus sighed. "Go ahead."

Hercules cleared his throat. "Okay. Chip, who is the most handsomest hero in all of Greece?" he asked.

"Apollo-ip!" Chip answered.

Zeus laughed. "Apollo! What answer were you expecting?"

Hercules frowned. "Okay, Chip, who is the *strongest* hero in all of Greece?"

"Era-hip," Chip replied. "E-ship as-hip e-thip trongest-sip ill-wip!"

Hercules looked at Zeus, confused.

"Hera, because she has the strongest will," Zeus told him. "I have to agree with that one."

Hercules tried again. "Okay, then who is the *smartest* hero in all of Greece?"

"I know that one," Zeus said. "It's Athena."

"Athena-ip!" Chip agreed.

Hercules shook his head. "I think Chip must be broken." He walked on, ahead of Zeus.

Their journey took them across the land bridge connecting northern and southern Greece. The turquoise waters of the Sea of Crete lapped against the shore, and tall grass sprouted from the sandy earth.

They walked all afternoon without having much conversation, and that was fine with Zeus. He sniffed the salt air and watched the white seagulls swooping against the blue sky. Every once in a while, Hercules would ask, "Are we there yet?" And Zeus would tell him no.

When the sun began to set, Zeus looked for a place to set up camp.

"There is a little grove of trees over there," Zeus said, pointing away from the shore. "We can start a fire."

"Wait, I see something," Hercules said, and he jogged toward a rocky outcrop along the coastline.

"Where are you going?" Zeus called out, following him. "We shouldn't sleep too close to the water. We'll get too cold!"

Hercules walked to the top of the outcrop. His eyes grew big. "It's a nest! Full of gold!"

Zeus caught up to him. The boy was right. A nest the size of a wagon wheel, made of straw and twigs, was nestled in the rocks, and inside the nest was a huge heap of gold coins.

Hercules reached and plucked a coin out of the nest. "We're rich!"

"Hercules, I wouldn't do that," Zeus warned. "I've seen enough monsters to know that anything with a nest that big isn't going to be friendly. Especially if you're stealing its coins."

"There's no mama bird in sight!" Hercules said, and he began to stuff the gold coins into his food pouch.

Zeus noticed that the coins were extra sparkly, in a familiar way. Could this have something to do with—

Screeeeeeeeeee!

A giant bird swooped down from the sky. It had the head of an eagle and yellow front legs with sharp talons. The back of it looked like a lion's body, with strong legs and sharp claws.

"Hercules, watch out!" Zeus yelled.

Hercules looked up and his eyes widened. But before he could run, the half eagle, half lion began to peck at the boy with its sharp beak.

"Ow! Ow! Ow!" Hercules complained.

"Drop the coins!" Zeus yelled.

"No way! I'm rich!" Hercules cried. He tried to bat away the creature with his bare hands.

Zeus sighed. He wasn't sure if Hercules deserved saving. But he couldn't stand by and watch him get pecked to death. He withdrew Bolt from his belt.

"Bolt, large!" he yelled.

Bolt sprang to its full size, sparking with electricity. Zeus carefully aimed it at the eagle-lion. He was about to let go of Bolt when a bubble floated in front of his face. Then he heard a voice behind him.

"Zeus! Don't hurt her!"

He turned to see his friend Aphrodite floating toward him on a cloud of bubbles.

CHAPTER SIX

A Sneak, a Liar, and a Thief

Zeus lowered Bolt.

"You know this bird?" Zeus asked.

"She's a griffin," Aphrodite explained. "A beautiful magical beast."

"Do you think you could ask her to stop pecking my friend?" Zeus asked.

Aphrodite frowned. "He's stealing. That's not very nice."

Zeus turned back to Hercules. "DROP

THE COINS!" he commanded, in a voice like thunder.

Hercules didn't argue this time. He opened the pouch and dumped the coins back into the nest.

"Griffy, stop!" Aphrodite called out.

The griffin stopped pecking at Hercules, and the boy wisely jumped away from the bird's nest.

Aphrodite approached the griffin and patted her head. Then she removed a golden apple from a pouch around her waist. She tossed the golden apple from one hand to the other, and gold coins appeared out of thin air and tumbled into the nest. Hercules's eyes got wide.

"Here you go, Griffy. Some more coins for you," Aphrodite said, and the creature made a happy cooing sound.

Then Aphrodite turned to Hercules. Zeus

had never seen Aphrodite angry before, but her blue eyes narrowed as she marched over to the boy, bubbles trailing behind her.

"Just what do you think you were doing?" she asked.

Hercules shrugged. "I saw some gold; I took the gold. What's the big deal?"

"That gold is Griffy's gold," Aphrodite said. "I gave it to her."

"I saw," Hercules said. "How would you like to invest in this pomegranate power drink I invented? Guaranteed to give you muscles!"

He flexed his arms for her.

"I can make all the gold I want, but I wouldn't give you a single coin!" Aphrodite told him. "Imagine, stealing coins from a help-less bird."

Hercules glanced over at the griffin's sharp

beak and powerful claws. "She doesn't look helpless."

Aphrodite spun around and faced Zeus. "Is he a friend of yours?"

"Not exactly," Zeus said. "He's on a quest, and I agreed to help him."

She frowned. "What kind of quest?"

"More like a punishment, actually," Zeus replied. "We're headed to the Lerna swamp to get a scale from the nine-headed Hydra."

Aphrodite smiled for the first time. "I guess you missed fighting monsters," she said.

"Yeah, I guess I did," he said. "Sorry about Griffy. I didn't realize she was your friend."

He looked over at the nest, where the griffin sat protectively on top of her pile of coins. Hercules was sneaking up behind the creature, trying to steal more. Zeus shot him a warning look and he backed off, sulking.

"That's okay about Griffy," Aphrodite replied. "She may be scary-looking, but she's good company out here."

"It must get lonely," Zeus remarked.

"I'm never lonely by the sea," Aphrodite said. "Now, there's a long way to go before you get to Lerna. Come over to my place for some food."

They followed the young goddess to a small hut set just off the beach. Inside, strings of seashells decorated the walls. She gave them bubbly water from a nearby spring, and bowls of fruit that looked like shiny jewels.

Zeus told Aphrodite about the humans and the silly problems they brought him, and Hercules made her laugh with a story about cleaning out the king's chicken coop. Her laughter sounded like a cascade of bells, filling the hut with tiny bubbles.

"We'd better get going," Zeus said, standing up. "There's a time limit on this task."

"Nice to meet you, Aphrodite," Hercules said, and gave her an exaggerated bow, which made her giggle. But when he straightened up, a golden apple rolled out from under his sleeve and bounced on the floor.

"Seriously?" she cried. "Stealing from a helpless bird wasn't enough for you. You had to steal from me, too!"

Hercules shrugged. "Honestly, I don't know where—"

Aphrodite held up her hand. "Just stop. Wait, don't bother to answer me. Whatever you say will be a lie."

She turned to Zeus. "You might want to think about who your friends are."

"I know he's a sneak and a liar and a thief," Zeus replied.

 55

"I'm not *that* bad," Hercules muttered.

Zeus ignored him. "But if he fails at his task, King Eurystheus will attack Olympus. That's why I'm helping him."

Aphrodite frowned. "Suit yourself. Just keep him away from me, please," she said.

"As soon as he's finished with his tasks, I hope to never see him again," Zeus replied.

Then Zeus and Hercules headed back to the path leading to the Hydra. Zeus waited until Aphrodite's hut was out of sight, and then he started yelling at Hercules.

"Why did you take her apple? She was being so nice to you, even after you tried to steal the gold coins!" Zeus asked.

"I couldn't help myself!" Hercules responded. "It was so gold, and so shiny, and it doesn't seem fair that you gods all have magical objects and I don't."

"Because you're not a god," Zeus reminded him.

"But I'm half god!" Hercules said. "That should count for something."

Zeus stopped. "Listen," he said. "Let's just find that Hydra, take the scale, and then get back home. After that, you're on your own."

"Fine!" Hercules said.

"Fine," Zeus answered.

After they set up camp for the night, they ate an evening meal of bread and cheese in silence around their campfire. They went to sleep without speaking. When Zeus woke up at sunrise, Hercules was awake and ready to go.

"Come on," he said. "Let's get this over with so you don't have to hang out with me anymore."

Hearing that, Zeus felt sorry for Hercules. *It's his own fault, though,* he told himself. *If*

he'd just stop being so dishonest, he might not be so bad.

They reached the end of the land bridge about an hour later. It was time to leave the sea and head inland to Lerna, where the Hydra lived in a big, swampy lake.

"Look, there's a nice shell," Hercules said, pointing to the water's edge. "I'm going to get it. Maybe I can give it to Aphrodite on the way back, as an apology."

"That's nice," Zeus said, and for the second time that day he wondered if he had been too hard on the boy.

As Hercules bent down to pick up the shell, the sand underneath his feet started to shake and quake. Hercules jumped back. Before he could run, an enormous crab erupted from the sand! The bright orange beast had two large, black-tipped front claws. Each of its beady eyes

was the size of one of the boys' heads. It picked up Hercules in one of its claws!

"Herc!" Zeus yelled. He raced across the sand and reached for his belt. "Bolt, large!"

But Bolt wasn't there.

Whoosh! The crab's claw swooped across the sand and snatched up Zeus. Now the beast had both boys in its grasp.

"Hercules, did you take Bolt from me?" Zeus asked.

"I just wanted to borrow it!" the boy called back. "To test it out!"

Zeus restrained himself from yelling at Hercules. They had a bigger problem. The crab was scuttling into the waves. Soon, they'd be submerged under the water, with no escape.

"Toss Bolt to me!" he cried.

Hercules struggled to move his arms. They were pinned to his sides, like Zeus's. "I can't!"

Zeus closed his eyes and tried to push the crab claw open. He kicked his feet. Nothing worked. He felt the cold water lapping at his feet. The crab was sinking deeper and deeper. Now the water was up to his neck.

Is this how it ends? he wondered. *Becoming some dinner for a giant crab?*

"Heeeeeeeeeeelp!" Zeus yelled.

CHAPTER SEVEN

The Promise

Zeus didn't stop trying to escape the crab's massive claw. He held his breath as the water covered his mouth. As it reached his nose, he could imagine Hera's voice in his head.

That's what you get for chasing after monsters!

Knowing Hera had been right was even worse than his impending doom. If he got out of this alive, he would . . .

Whoosh! A huge wave rose up unexpectedly,

lifting the crab and its two prisoners out of the water. The wave deposited the creature back on the sandy shore with a thud.

"As Lord of the Sea, I command thee, crab! Unhand them!"

The crab's claws opened up, sending Zeus and Hercules tumbling onto the sand. As the crab scuttled back into the water, Zeus leaped to his feet and charged Hercules.

"Give me back Bolt, now!" he demanded.

"What, aren't you going to say thank you?"

Zeus spun around. His brother Poseidon stood on the shore. His wavy black hair was damp with seawater, and his turquoise eyes were the same color as the ocean. He held a three-pronged trident in one hand, and tucked under one arm was a long, smooth wooden board, with rounded edges.

"Thanks!" Zeus said. "Sorry, Poseidon. I

could have gotten us out of that mess if this guy hadn't stolen Bolt."

He held out his hand and Hercules placed the lightning-shaped dagger in Zeus's palm.

"And who is this guy?" Poseidon asked.

"Poseidon, Hercules," Zeus said. "Hercules, this is my brother Poseidon."

"Nice to meet you," Hercules said. "Although I was just about to wrestle that crab to the ocean floor and rescue myself and Zeus."

Poseidon grinned. "Flipping fish sticks, you sure know how to tell a whopper, dude!" he said. "That crab was about to chow down on you."

"I was waiting for the right moment to attack," Hercules said, and Poseidon laughed.

"So, did you guys come to visit, or what? We could hang out," he said, and he nodded toward the board under his arm. "I invented this thing where you take a flat piece of wood, and you polish it, and then you stand on it and ride the waves. It's awesome. I call it 'wave riding.'"

"That does sound awesome," Zeus said. "It sounds like you're having fun, you know, being Lord of the Sea and all."

"It's not bad," Poseidon agreed. "It gets a little bit lonely. I mean, I can communicate with sea creatures and stuff, but most of them don't have anything interesting to say. A lot of fish just want to know where the algae is, or how to avoid getting eaten by other fish."

Zeus nodded. "They kind of sound like the villagers in Athens. They're always bringing me their problems."

Poseidon playfully punched Zeus on the shoulder. "Looks like you and this liar dude are on some kind of adventure, though. That's pretty cool."

Zeus explained the story of Hercules and the three tasks.

"So we're on our way to get a scale from the Hydra, and then the first task will be complete," Zeus told him. "Hey, you could come with us! It'll be just like when we went on those quests that Pythia sent us on."

Poseidon shook his head. "Sorry, Bro, can't help you," he said. "The Hydra is an ancient beast who's been around for a long, long time. She was scaring all the sailors in the sea, so I made a deal with her and found a sweet swamp for her to hang out in. She stays there, and I promised that I wouldn't let anybody bother her. She gets a bad rap with those nine heads of hers. But she can't help it if she's hungry all the time!"

Zeus nodded. "Okay. I get why you can't come."

Poseidon frowned. "You won't hurt her, will you? Because I promised her nobody would bug her. That's our deal."

"How are we supposed to promise that?" Hercules asked. "What if she tries to eat us?"

Poseidon looked thoughtful. "She sleeps a lot," he said. "Just wait until she's sleeping, pluck out a scale, and then hurry out of there."

Zeus nodded. "Sounds like a plan."

"Sure," Hercules said.

"Cool," Poseidon said. "Catch you later, Bro and Liar Dude!"

Then he walked into the water and dropped the board. He lay facedown on it and paddled into the sea. Right before a big wave approached, he stood up on the board. Zeus and Hercules watched as the wave carried him away.

Zeus turned to Hercules, his eyes flashing. "Never. Take. Bolt. AGAIN!" he demanded, and thunder rumbled across the beach.

CHAPTER EIGHT

The Monster
in the Swamp

Hercules took a step back from Zeus, holding up his hands. "Okay, okay, chill!" he said. "I won't touch Bolt again. I won't even look at it."

Zeus calmed down a little bit. "I don't understand you," he said. "If you're a mighty half god, like you say, then why do you keep stealing magical stuff? You're probably lying about that, too."

"I am *not*," Hercules insisted. "My mom told me, and she doesn't lie. My dad disappeared before I was born, but she said he had mighty powers. And when I was a baby, two snakes crawled into my cradle. When Mom came to check on me, she said I had tied the two snakes into a knot!"

It sounds like his mom's a liar too, Zeus thought.

"So you've never met your dad?" Zeus asked.

"Nope," Hercules said. "I was raised by my mom and my aunts. And they told me I was the strongest, smartest, handsomest boy in all of Greece!"

Zeus rolled his eyes. No wonder Hercules had such a big opinion of himself, if his head was being filled with huge compliments all the time.

He felt a little pang of jealousy at Hercules's

story too. Zeus's own father, King Cronus, had tried to swallow him when he was born. His mother, Rhea, had replaced baby Zeus with a rock wrapped in a blanket. Cronus had swallowed the rock, and Rhea had brought Zeus into the woods and left him there. He hadn't met either of them until he began his quest to become an Olympian.

"Well, good for you," Zeus replied. "I was raised mainly by goats and bees, and they didn't have a whole lot to say."

"Goats and bees? Cool," Hercules said. "What was that like?"

"Forget it," Zeus said. "I just hope your mighty half-god powers come in handy when we're facing a nine-headed monster."

Zeus didn't feel like talking. He turned away from Hercules and headed for the path.

They made their way away from the sea,

following a thin stream that led into a murky forest. The air smelled different to Zeus—salty, like the ocean, but with the odor of rotting plants, too. The ground underneath their feet felt squishy.

"This must be the swamp," Zeus guessed, speaking for the first time in hours. "Chip, where will we find the Hydra?"

A green arrow glowed on Chip's smooth surface, pointing west. Zeus held Chip in his hand, following the arrow through the swamp. They wove through trees with twisted trunks and low-hanging branches. Leaves brushed against the boys' faces as they walked. Zeus couldn't see any animals, but strange croaks and chirps accompanied them with each step.

Finally they reached a large lake filled with brown, murky water. Insects buzzed across the surface. Across the lake was a low, tree-covered hill. The mouth of a cave opened up in the hill, right by the lake's shore.

They stopped and stared at the water.

"Do you think she's under there, somewhere?" Hercules asked.

"Maybe," Zeus said, and then he nodded toward the cave. "More likely she lives in there. We should check it out."

"So, you've fought monsters like the Hydra before?" Hercules asked in a whisper as they made their way around the lake.

"Not exactly like the Hydra," Zeus replied. "Some were just strange, like those warriors who hopped around on one foot. The Titans had really strong powers. And that last dragon we fought was massive. Every time one of its teeth fell out, more warriors sprang from the ground! It took all of us to defeat him."

"Do you think the two of us can take the Hydra?" Hercules asked.

"We're not going to fight her," Zeus reminded him. "We're going to wait until she's asleep, pull out a scale, and run."

They reached the mouth of the cave. Zeus peered into the darkness. The lake continued inside the cave, rimmed by an earthen walkway. Sunlight glittered off some object in the back of the cave.

"I don't see the Hydra," Hercules said.

Zeus put a finger to his lips and slowly entered the cave. The sunlight glittered on the water, too, and on the surface were several green, round bumps sticking out. They looked to Zeus like mossy rocks.

Zeus squinted, studying the bumps, as Hercules pushed past him to inspect the glittery pile in the back of the cave. Zeus counted the bumps. One, two, three, four, five, six, seven, eight, nine.

He stepped closer to the water's edge. Little bubbles popped up in front of each of the bumps. And the green wasn't moss at all, but looked like scales—shiny green scales. The hairs on his arms stood up. These were the nine heads of the Hydra! The creature was sleeping underwater, her heads sticking up on top of the surface.

Those bubbles must be from her breathing, Zeus guessed. He quickly formulated a plan. He could dive into the pond while Hercules kept watch. If he approached the Hydra from behind, he could peel a scale off her body without her noticing, just like Poseidon had said.

What are you thinking? Let Hercules do the swimming, Zeus told himself.

He turned to tell Hercules the plan, but the boy wasn't there. Then he heard a clinking sound in the back of the cave.

Now that his eyes had adjusted to the dim light, he could make out the source of the glittering light—a huge treasure pile! Hercules was climbing through it, tossing aside golden goblets and jeweled crowns.

"Hercules, get down!" Zeus called out in a harsh whisper.

Hercules didn't listen. He picked up a huge sword and held it up. The sword's sharp, silver blade gleamed, and Hercules grinned. Then he let out a war cry.

"Aaaaaaaaaaaaaah!" He charged down from the treasure pile, swinging the sword over his head.

CHAPTER NINE

Ten Angry Heads

All eighteen yellow eyes of the Hydra snapped open. All nine heads shot out of the water on long necks. Nine red tongues unfurled from nine angry, squealing mouths.

"Hercules, no!" Zeus yelled. "We promised Poseidon we wouldn't hurt her!"

"Hercules the Mighty is not afraid of any monster!" the boy shouted, and he charged into the water, wildly swinging the sword.

All nine heads shot out streams of green poison. By some miracle, they avoided hitting Hercules. He swung the blade again, and one of the Hydra heads went flying and landed in the treasure pile.

"Take that!" Hercules cheered.

Zeus gasped. "No!" he cried. What had Hercules done?

He flinched and started to turn away, but stopped. Two brand-new hissing Hydra heads sprouted from the neck that Hercules had attacked. Now the Hydra had ten heads instead of nine!

Hercules raised the sword over his head again. *He doesn't realize he's just making it worse!* Zeus thought. He knew he had to act fast. But what could he do?

His first instinct was to stop Hercules. He tossed Bolt at the boy and knocked the sword away from him. Bolt circled back around and landed in Zeus's hand.

"Hey!" Hercules protested.

The Hydra reared back all ten heads, preparing another poison attack.

"Hercules, look out!" Zeus warned.

Hercules jumped into the treasure pile as the sizzling green poison shot from the Hydra's ten mouths. The beast was on its feet now, revealing an enormous, lizard-like body covered in shimmering green scales.

The creature still hadn't seen Zeus. He could have run out of the cave without looking back. But he couldn't leave Hercules behind—even if everything was the boy's fault.

"Bolt, large!"

Bolt grew to its full size, and Zeus thrust it into the water. Ripples of electricity zapped the Hydra. All ten heads spun around and saw Zeus.

Uh-oh! Zeus thought.

"Hercules, get out while you can!" he yelled. "I'll distract her!"

Hercules tumbled out of the treasure pile and raced around the walkway, behind the Hydra. Zeus struck the Hydra with Bolt, zapping her directly, before she could aim a poison blast at him. The Hydra's body sizzled and she shrieked, but two of her heads still managed to shoot out poison streams. Zeus dodged them, ending up farther back inside the cave.

Whomp! Zeus felt his legs give out as the Hydra whacked him hard behind the knees with one of her heads. He skidded across the cave floor, and Bolt flew out of his hands.

"Bolt, return!" Zeus yelled, and Bolt flew toward him just as another spray of green poison shot from the Hydra. Zeus tumbled out of the way, missing his chance to catch Bolt.

Whomp! The Hydra whacked Zeus again, sending him flying into the back wall of the cave. He bounced off and landed on the pile of treasure. As he got to his knees, he found himself face-to-face with the Hydra head that Hercules had chopped off.

"Aaaaaaaah!" Zeus cried, jumping back, but that was the least of his worries. All ten heads were trained on him now, and he had nowhere to run.

At least Hercules got away, he thought. But then he heard the boy's voice echo through the cave.

"I am Hercules the Mighty!"

Hercules was behind the Hydra, gripping the creature's thick tail. With a powerful heave, he pulled the beast backward, away from Zeus!

Startled, all ten heads turned to look at Hercules. Seeing his chance, Zeus sprinted down from the treasure pile and raced toward the mouth of the cave, picking up Bolt on his way.

Drops of green poison rained down inside the cave as the Hydra tried to attack. Hercules faced the Hydra and raised his sword.

"No!" Zeus yelled. He grabbed Hercules. "We need to run!"

They raced out of the cave, around the lake, and back into the swamp. They didn't stop until they had to catch their breath.

"We . . . escaped . . . ," Hercules said, panting.

"We did," Zeus said. "But there's one problem."

"What's that?" Hercules asked.

Zeus groaned. "We didn't get a scale from the Hydra!"

CHAPTER TEN

Brothers and Enemies

Hercules's face fell. "Oh, okay. So I guess we should go back?"

Zeus frowned. "We'll need a plan this time. Maybe we should . . ." He spotted something on Hercules's tunic. Something green and shiny. He picked it up.

"Herc, look!" he said. "It's a scale from the Hydra! It must have fallen off her tail when you were dragging her around!" Excited, he shook the other boy's shoulder.

Hercules looked at the scale and grinned. "Yeah! I did it!"

Zeus stopped. "*You* did it? Are you serious?"

"Yeah," Hercules replied. "You were trapped in the back of the cave, and I used my superstrength to pull the Hydra away so you could escape. And then I got a scale off her tail."

Back in the cave, Zeus hadn't had time to think about how Hercules really *did* have superstrength. No ordinary kid could have handled the Hydra like that. He hadn't been lying about that after all. But everything else he'd just said . . .

"The only reason I was trapped in the back of the cave was because *I* had to save *you*," Zeus shot back. "We had a plan, and you didn't stick with it! And also, you didn't take the scale off the Hydra's tail. You're lucky one fell off and got stuck on your tunic."

"Yes, but I saved us in the end," Hercules insisted. "Hercules the Mighty saves the day!"

Fuming, Zeus turned his back on Hercules and marched through the swamp. Hercules followed him.

"Do you think Apollo will write a song about my incredible feat of strength?" Hercules wondered. "I bet he will. I bet it will be a big hit."

Zeus shook his head. "Let's just get back to Delphi, okay?"

Hercules shrugged. "Sure!"

They made their way through the swamp. When they returned to the coast, they found Poseidon waiting for them, holding his trident. He looked angry.

"You promised!" he said. "You promised not

to hurt the Hydra, and then you went and cut off one of her heads! And zapped her with Bolt!"

Zeus winced. "I tried to stop him," he said. "We had a plan, but Hercules—"

"Hercules is just a dude, and you are an Olympian," Poseidon pointed out. "You should have been in control of the situation, Bro. And *you* hurt her too. You were the one who zapped her."

"I had to," Zeus said. "I had to do it so we could get away. I'm sorry, I really am."

"I don't see what the big deal is," Hercules said. "I mean, she should thank me. Now she has one *extra* head. Aren't ten heads better than nine?"

Both Poseidon and Zeus glared at Hercules. Poseidon walked to the water and stuck his trident in it. When he pulled it out, a bubble began to form on the end of one of the prongs.

The bubble grew until it was twice as big as the boy's head.

He tapped it, and an image of the Hydra appeared. She was curled up on the top of her treasure pile. All ten heads looked sad.

"She *misses* that head, and now she's mad at me," Poseidon said. "I don't know how I'm going to keep her out of the ocean now. It's a big problem, and it's all *your* fault." He said this to Zeus, not to Hercules.

"I'm really sorry," Zeus said. "Listen, we need to get back to Delphi right away. But when I'm done, I'll come back and help you. Okay?"

"Whatever," Poseidon mumbled, and Zeus knew his brother was really upset.

Zeus walked away without another word. Hercules followed him.

"Zeus," he began.

"I have nothing to say to you," Zeus said.

"Hera was right. I never should have come on this trip with you. Now Poseidon is angry with me, and he and I used to be . . . we were more than brothers. We were best friends."

"I just wanted to say that I'm sorry," Hercules said.

Zeus stopped. It was the first time he'd ever heard the boy apologize, and he sounded like he meant it.

"I'm really glad you came with me," Hercules went on. "I shouldn't have hurt the Hydra like that. I guess I was just . . . scared. And I didn't want you to know."

"It's normal to be scared of monsters," Zeus told him.

"Normal for people, but not half gods," Hercules replied.

"It's normal for half gods and full gods," Zeus said. "Me and the other Olympians were always afraid. But we knew we had each other to count on."

Hercules grinned. "Just like you and me, Zeus, right?"

"Not exactly," Zeus said. He started walking. "Come on, we've got to get back to the temple before the deadline."

He and Hercules made the three-day journey back to Delphi. They didn't see Aphrodite on their way back, and Zeus thought that was for the best. She was upset with him too.

Tired and dirty from the road, they reached the temple at Delphi exactly one week after the task began. Inside, they found Pythia and Apollo waiting for them, along with Hera. King Eurystheus was there, flanked by four soldiers. His face fell when Zeus and Hercules walked in.

"You're alive," he said in a flat voice.

"Yes, we are," Hercules said, pushing in front

of Zeus. "And behold, Hercules the Mighty has brought you the scale of the beastly, ten-headed Hydra, with the help of his assistant, Zeus!"

Zeus glared at Hercules. "Assistant?"

Hera chimed in. "I thought it was a nine-headed Hydra."

"Not anymore!" Hercules replied.

"Where is this° scale?" the king wanted to know.

Zeus removed it from his pouch and handed it to the king. Everyone leaned in to examine the shimmering scale.

"That looks like a Hydra scale to me," Pythia confirmed.

"Excellent!" Hercules said. "And now I'll just be heading back to my mom. Unless, Apollo, you want to write a song about my adventures. Then I can hang around for a bit."

"Never mind the song," King Eurystheus said. "You still need to do two more tasks. That was the deal!"

"Fine, fine, two more tasks," Hercules said. "Now that I've defeated the Hydra, any other task you give me will be a piece of cake!"

"Okay, then," Apollo said. "Let me look into the future. Pythia?"

Pythia waved her arms around, and the mist rose up in the temple. Apollo gazed into the mist for a few minutes, and then began to strum his lyre.

"Hercules has brought the Hydra's scale,
But that is part one of this tale.
Now it is time for task number two,
And here is what young Herc must do:
Travel to the Amazon land so green,
And get the belt from the warrior queen."

Apollo stopped playing, and the fog cleared.

"I remember the Amazons," Zeus said. "They're tough, but they're nice."

"They're awesome," Hera added.

"Get a belt from a lady warrior?" Hercules asked. He laughed. "That is no challenge for Hercules the Mighty!"

"I wouldn't be so sure of that," Hera told him.

Hercules ignored her. "I'll leave right away! I can do this one all by myself."

"Fine," Zeus said. "I didn't want to go with you anyway."

Hercules waved to them all. "I am off! I will return in a week."

He left the temple.

Hera looked at Zeus. "Are you sure you want him to go alone?"

Zeus shrugged. "You heard him. He can do

this by himself. He took care of the Hydra, didn't he?"

Hera looked in his eyes. "Did he? Or did he mess everything up, and you had to save him?"

Hercules was making his way down the steps of the temple. "No time for autographs! Hercules the Mighty is on a quest!"

Zeus frowned. If Zeus hadn't gone with him, Hercules would have been gobbled up by a Hydra head by now.

Hercules was a liar, a braggart, a thief, and an annoying traveling companion. Even so, Zeus didn't want anything bad to happen to the boy. Besides, Hercules still had two more tasks to finish. If he failed (and he probably would), King Eurystheus would wage war on Olympus.

He sighed. "Wait up, Hercules!" he called out, and he headed down the temple stairs.